REBEL'S REPORT

ROGUE ONE: VOLUME 5

OPERATIVES:

Jyn Erso and Rebel Intelligence officer Cassian Andor have disobeyed direct orders and assembled a ragtag group of rebel fighters in order to infiltrate the Imperial base on Scarif.

JYN ERSO

CAPTAIN CASSIAN ANDOR

MISSION:

Steal the Death Star plans and reveal the strategic weakness within the weapon, placed there by scientist Galen Erso (deceased).

GALEN ERSO

NOTES:

Galen Erso, Imperial scientist and father of Jyn Erso, was killed during a Rebel raid on an Imperial base, although not before Imperial Director Krennic discovered Galen's treason.

ORSON KRENNIC

CREDITS:

WRITER	Jody Houser
ARTIST	Emilio Laiso
COLORIST	Rachelle Rosenberg
LETTERER	VC's Clayton Cowles
COVER ARTIST	Phil Noto
PRODUCTION DESIGN	Carlos Lao
EDITOR	Heather Antos
SUPERVISING EDITOR	Jordan D. White
EXECUTIVE EDITOR	C.B. Cebulski
EDITOR IN CHIEF	Axel Alonso
CHIEF CREATIVE OFFICER	Joe Quesada
PRESIDENT	Dan Buckley
EXECUTIVE PRODUCER	Alan Fine

Based on the screenplay by Chris Weitz and Tony Gilroy

Based on a story by John Knoll and Gary Whitta

LUCASFILM:

SENIOR EDITOR	Frank Parisi
CREATIVE DIRECTOR	Michael Siglain
LUCASFILM STORY GROUP	James Waugh, Leland Chee, Matt Martin, Rayne Roberts

marvelkids.com

Spotlight

ABDOPUBLISHING.COM

Reinforced library bound edition published in 2019 by Spotlight,
a division of ABDO, PO Box 398166, Minneapolis, Minnesota 55439.
Spotlight produces high-quality reinforced library bound editions for
schools and libraries. Published by agreement with Marvel Characters, Inc.

Printed in the United States of America, North Mankato, Minnesota.
042018
092018

THIS BOOK CONTAINS
RECYCLED MATERIALS

STAR WARS © & TM 2018 LUCASFILM LTD.

Library of Congress Control Number: 2017961400

Publisher's Cataloging in Publication Data

Names: Houser, Jody, author. | Laiso, Emilio; Bazaldua, Oscar; Rosenberg, Rachelle;
    Villanelli, Paolo, illustrators.
Title: Rogue One / writer: Jody Houser; art: Emilio Laiso, Oscar Bazaldua, Rachelle
    Rosenberg, and Paolo Villanelli.
Description: Reinforced library bound edition. | Minneapolis, MN : Spotlight, 2019 |
    Series: Star Wars: Rogue One | Volume 1 written by Jody Houser; illustrated
    by Emilio Laiso, Oscar Bazaldua and Rachelle Rosenberg. | Volumes 2, 4, 5,
    and 6 written by Jody Houser; illustrated by Emilio Laiso and Rachelle
    Rosenberg. | Volume 3 written by Jody Houser; illustrated by Paolo Villanelli
    and Rachelle Rosenberg.
Summary: Scientist Galen Erso is taken from his home and forced to work on the
    Empire's secret planet-killing weapon, leaving his daughter, Jyn, to grow up
    on her own. Fifteen years later, Galen leaks information on the weapon, through
    a message he sends to some bandits on the moon Jedha. Now, the rebels of
    the Alliance want to know if the rumors of an Imperial Death Star are true.
    They'll need Jyn to help retrieve the message and, possibly, find her father.
Identifiers: ISBN 9781532141683 (Volume 1) | ISBN 9781532141690 (Volume
    2) | ISBN 9781532141706 (Volume 3) | ISBN 9781532141713 (Volume 4) | ISBN
    9781532141720 (Volume 5) | ISBN 9781532141737 (Volume 6)
Subjects: LCSH: Star Wars films--Juvenile fiction. | Weapons--Juvenile fiction. |
    Space colonies--Juvenile fiction. | Imaginary wars and battles--Juvenile fiction. |
    Comic books, strips, etc.--Juvenile fiction.
Classification: DDC 741.5--dc23

3 2872 50152 8180

Spotlight

A Division of ABDO
abdopublishing.com

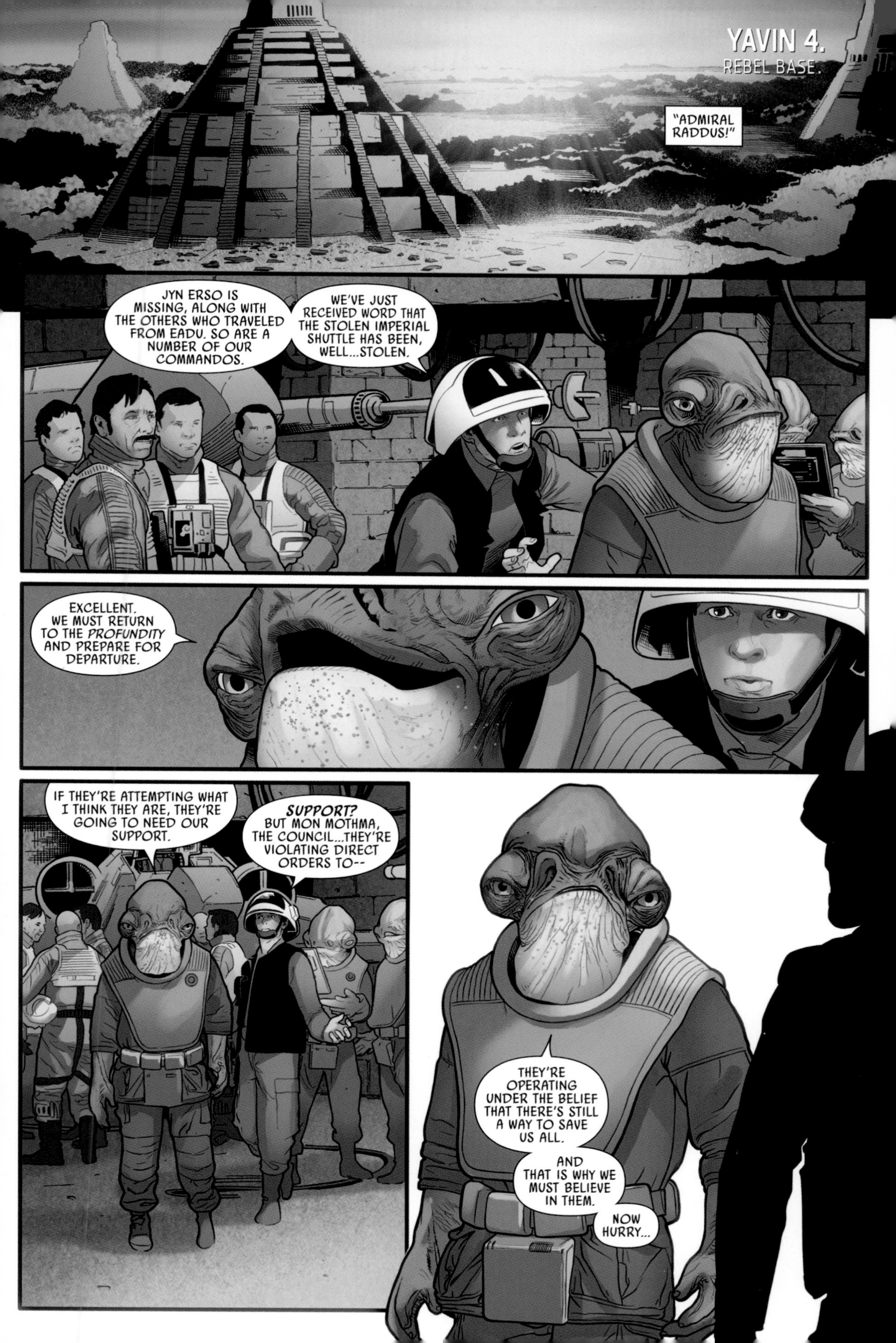
YAVIN 4.
REBEL BASE.
"ADMIRAL RADDUS!"
JYN ERSO IS MISSING, ALONG WITH THE OTHERS WHO TRAVELED FROM EADU. SO ARE A NUMBER OF OUR COMMANDOS.
WE'VE JUST RECEIVED WORD THAT THE STOLEN IMPERIAL SHUTTLE HAS BEEN, WELL...STOLEN.
EXCELLENT. WE MUST RETURN TO THE *PROFUNDITY* AND PREPARE FOR DEPARTURE.
IF THEY'RE ATTEMPTING WHAT I THINK THEY ARE, THEY'RE GOING TO NEED OUR SUPPORT.
SUPPORT? BUT MON MOTHMA, THE COUNCIL...THEY'RE VIOLATING DIRECT ORDERS TO--
THEY'RE OPERATING UNDER THE BELIEF THAT THERE'S STILL A WAY TO SAVE US ALL.
AND THAT IS WHY WE MUST BELIEVE IN THEM.
NOW HURRY...

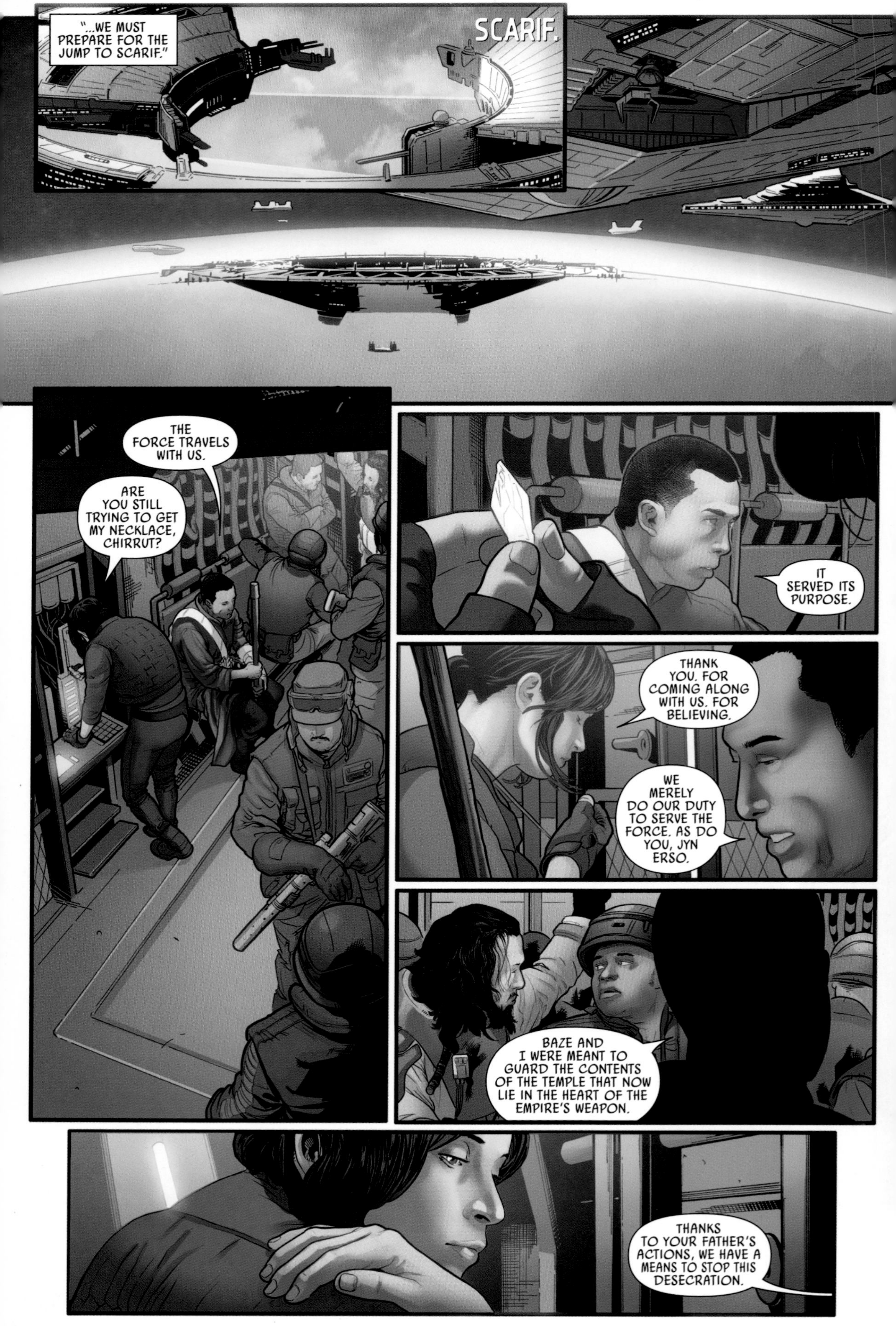

"...WE MUST PREPARE FOR THE JUMP TO SCARIF."
SCARIF.
THE FORCE TRAVELS WITH US.
ARE YOU STILL TRYING TO GET MY NECKLACE, CHIRRUT?
IT SERVED ITS PURPOSE.
THANK YOU. FOR COMING ALONG WITH US. FOR BELIEVING.
WE MERELY DO OUR DUTY TO SERVE THE FORCE. AS DO YOU, JYN ERSO.
BAZE AND I WERE MEANT TO GUARD THE CONTENTS OF THE TEMPLE THAT NOW LIE IN THE HEART OF THE EMPIRE'S WEAPON.
THANKS TO YOUR FATHER'S ACTIONS, WE HAVE A MEANS TO STOP THIS DESECRATION.

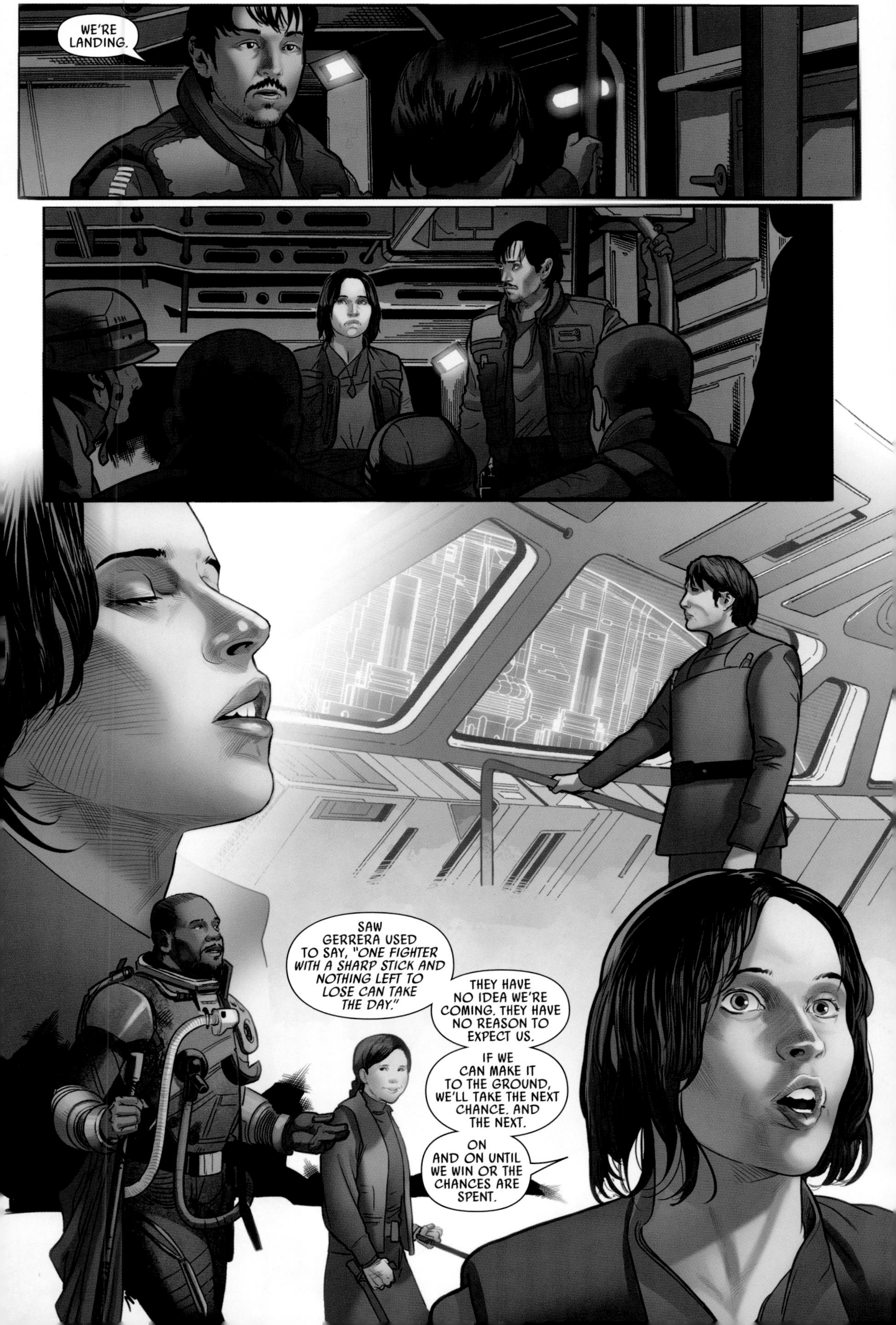
WE'RE LANDING.
SAW GERRERA USED TO SAY, "ONE FIGHTER WITH A SHARP STICK AND NOTHING LEFT TO LOSE CAN TAKE THE DAY."
THEY HAVE NO IDEA WE'RE COMING. THEY HAVE NO REASON TO EXPECT US.
IF WE CAN MAKE IT TO THE GROUND, WE'LL TAKE THE NEXT CHANCE. AND THE NEXT.
ON AND ON UNTIL WE WIN OR THE CHANCES ARE SPENT.

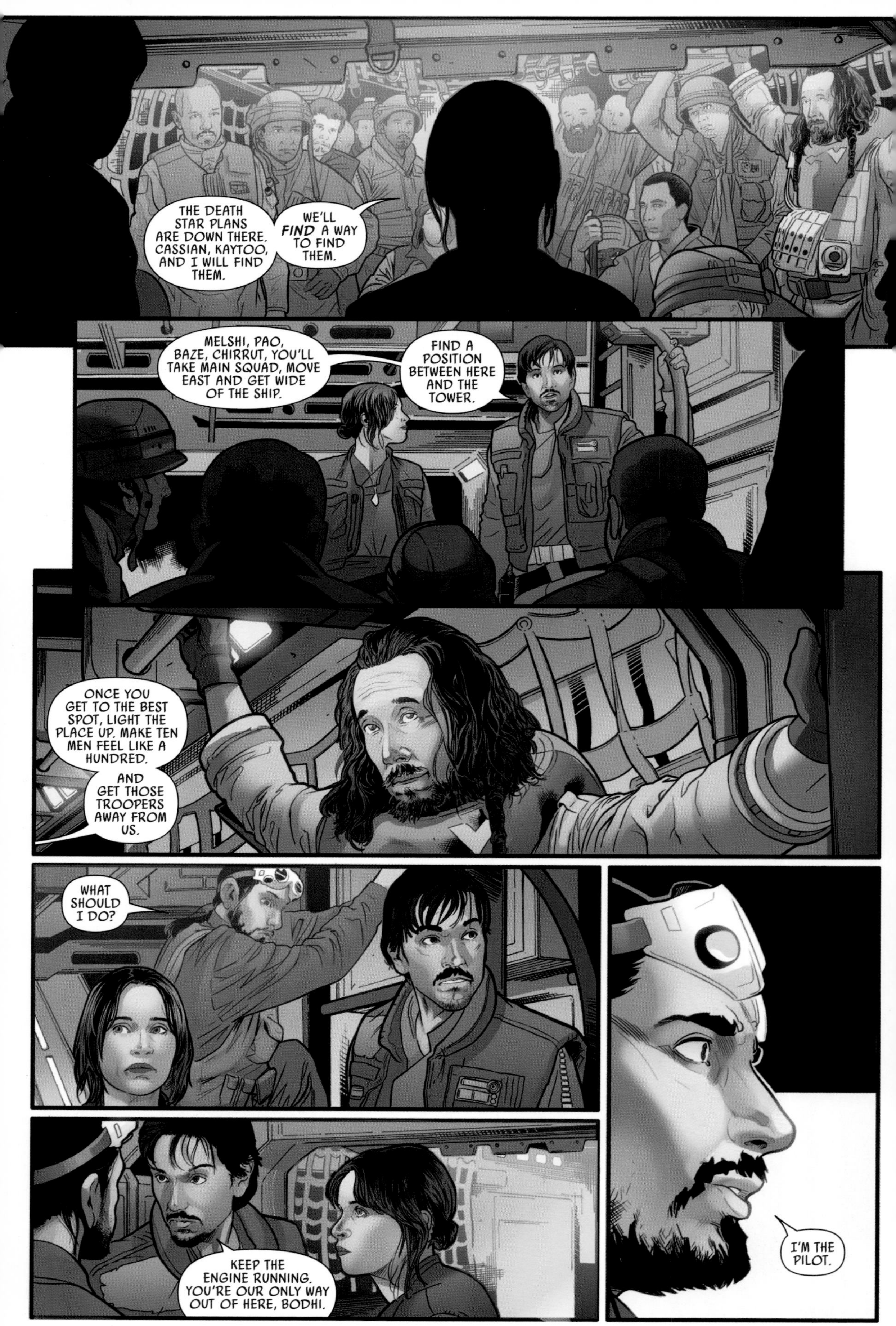
THE DEATH STAR PLANS ARE DOWN THERE. CASSIAN, KAYTOO, AND I WILL FIND THEM.
WE'LL **FIND** A WAY TO FIND THEM.
MELSHI, PAO, BAZE, CHIRRUT, YOU'LL TAKE MAIN SQUAD, MOVE EAST AND GET WIDE OF THE SHIP.
FIND A POSITION BETWEEN HERE AND THE TOWER.
ONCE YOU GET TO THE BEST SPOT, LIGHT THE PLACE UP. MAKE TEN MEN FEEL LIKE A HUNDRED.
AND GET THOSE TROOPERS AWAY FROM US.
WHAT SHOULD I DO?
KEEP THE ENGINE RUNNING. YOU'RE OUR ONLY WAY OUT OF HERE, BODHI.
I'M THE PILOT.

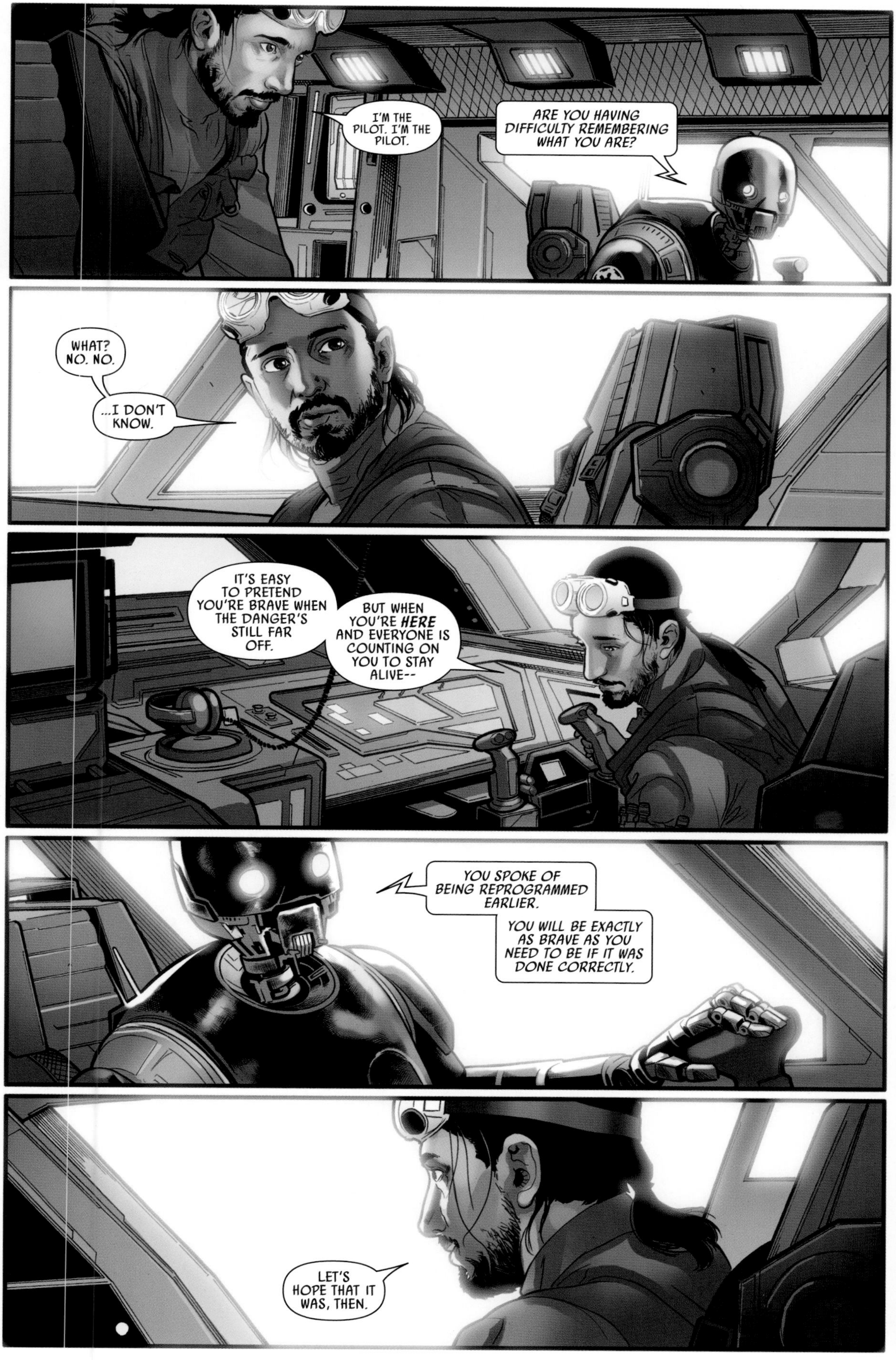
I'M THE PILOT. I'M THE PILOT.
ARE YOU HAVING DIFFICULTY REMEMBERING WHAT YOU ARE?
WHAT? NO. NO.
...I DON'T KNOW.
IT'S EASY TO PRETEND YOU'RE BRAVE WHEN THE DANGER'S STILL FAR OFF.
BUT WHEN YOU'RE *HERE* AND EVERYONE IS COUNTING ON YOU TO STAY ALIVE--
YOU SPOKE OF BEING REPROGRAMMED EARLIER.
YOU WILL BE EXACTLY AS BRAVE AS YOU NEED TO BE IF IT WAS DONE CORRECTLY.
LET'S HOPE THAT IT WAS, THEN.

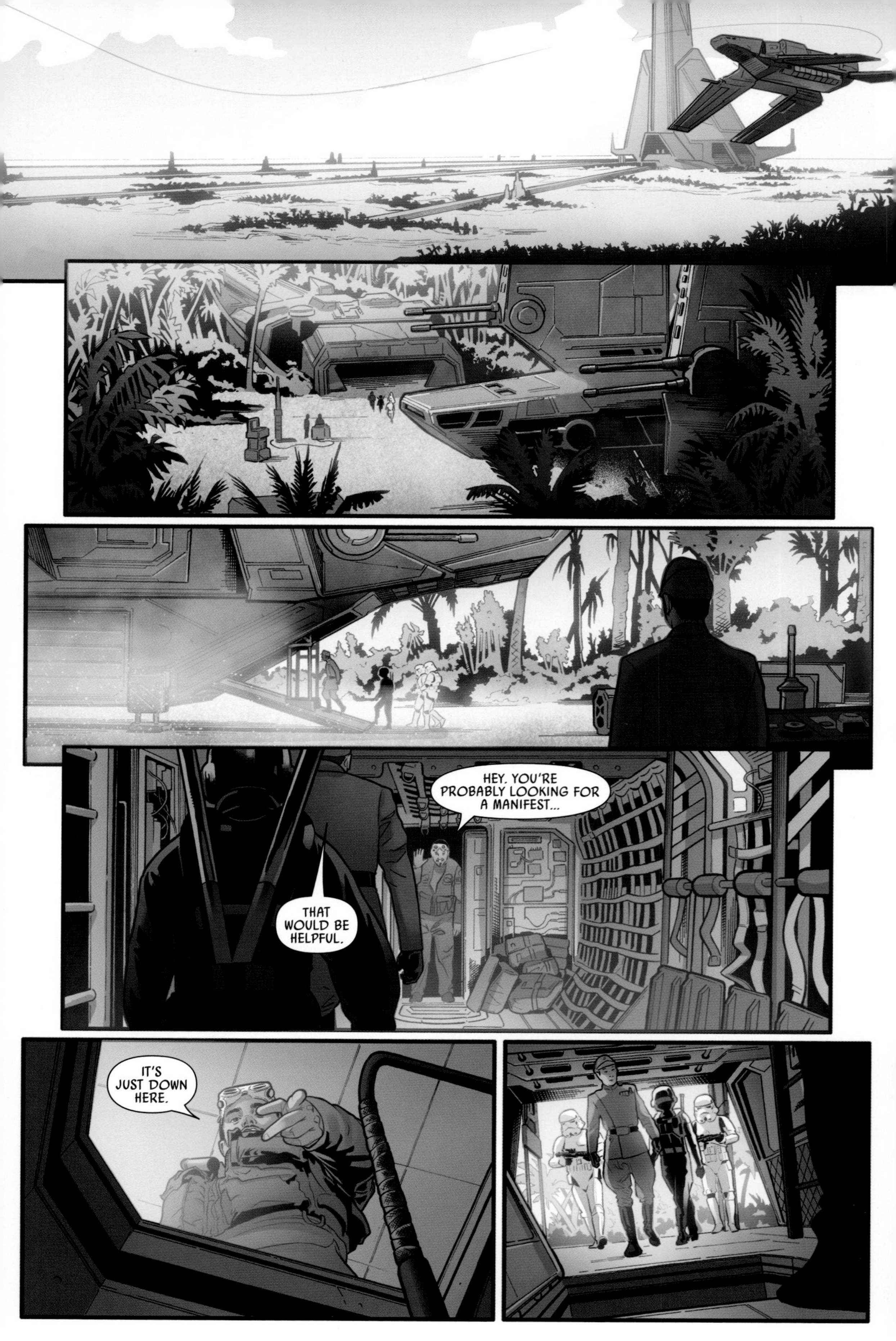
HEY. YOU'RE PROBABLY LOOKING FOR A MANIFEST...
THAT WOULD BE HELPFUL.
IT'S JUST DOWN HERE.

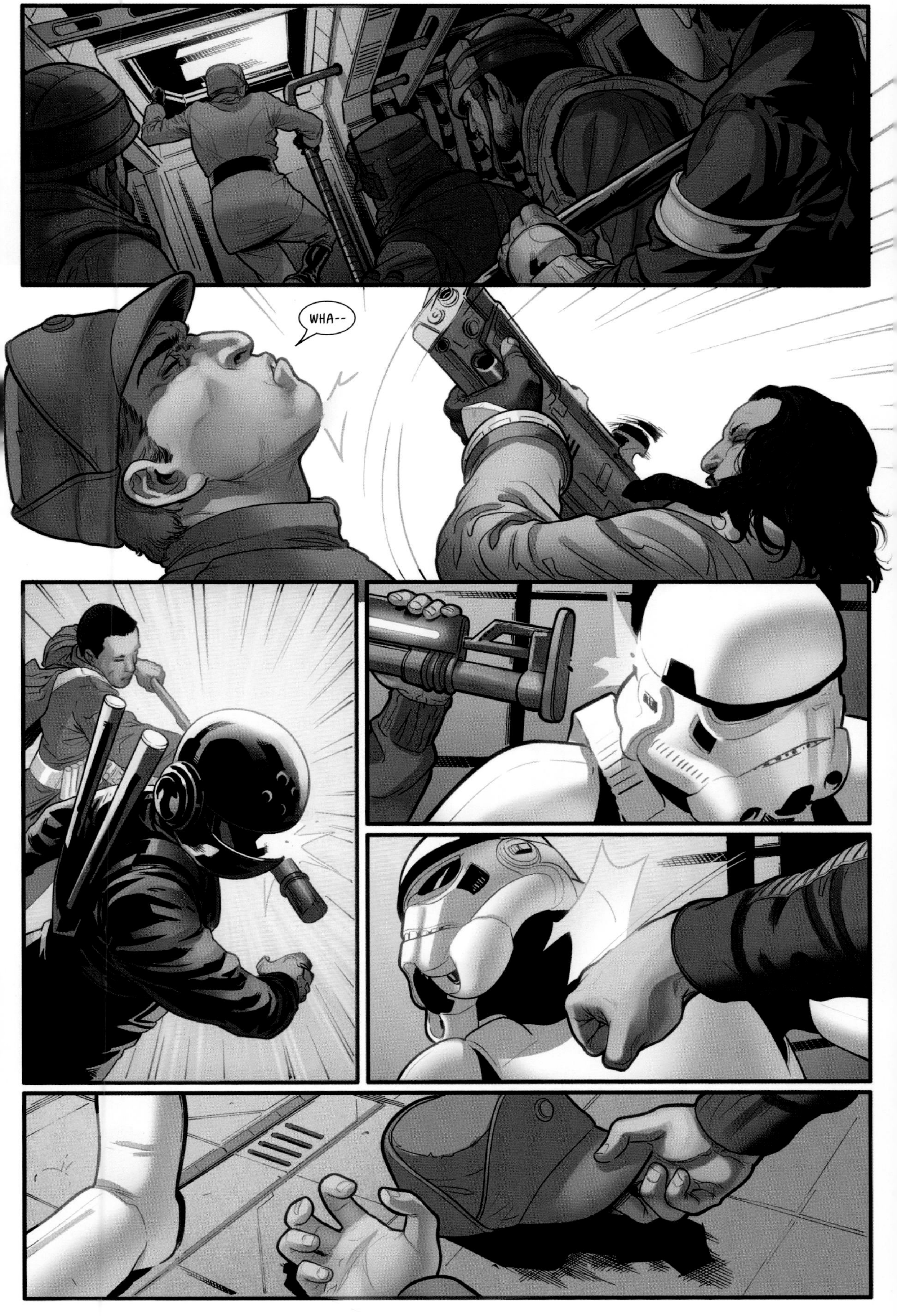
WHA--

GOOD LUCK, LITTLE SISTER.

GO, GO NOW! YOU'RE CLEAR!

I'VE GOT A BAD FEELING ABOUT--

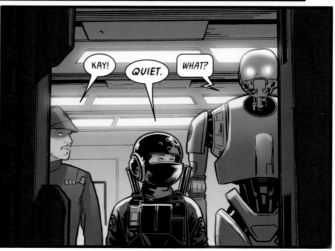

KAY!

QUIET.

WHAT?

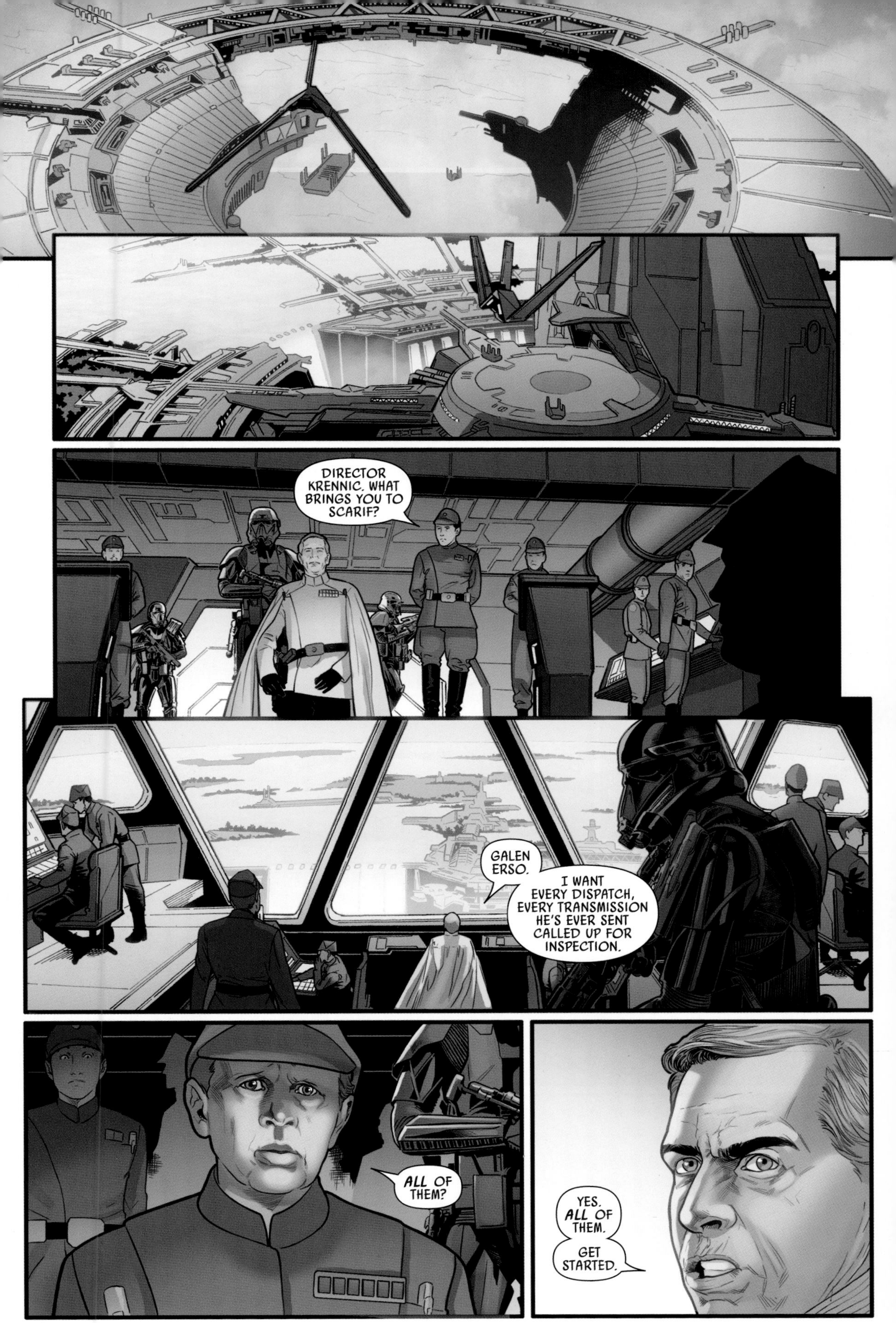
DIRECTOR KRENNIC. WHAT BRINGS YOU TO SCARIF?
GALEN ERSO.
I WANT EVERY DISPATCH, EVERY TRANSMISSION HE'S EVER SENT CALLED UP FOR INSPECTION.
ALL OF THEM?
YES. ALL OF THEM.
GET STARTED.

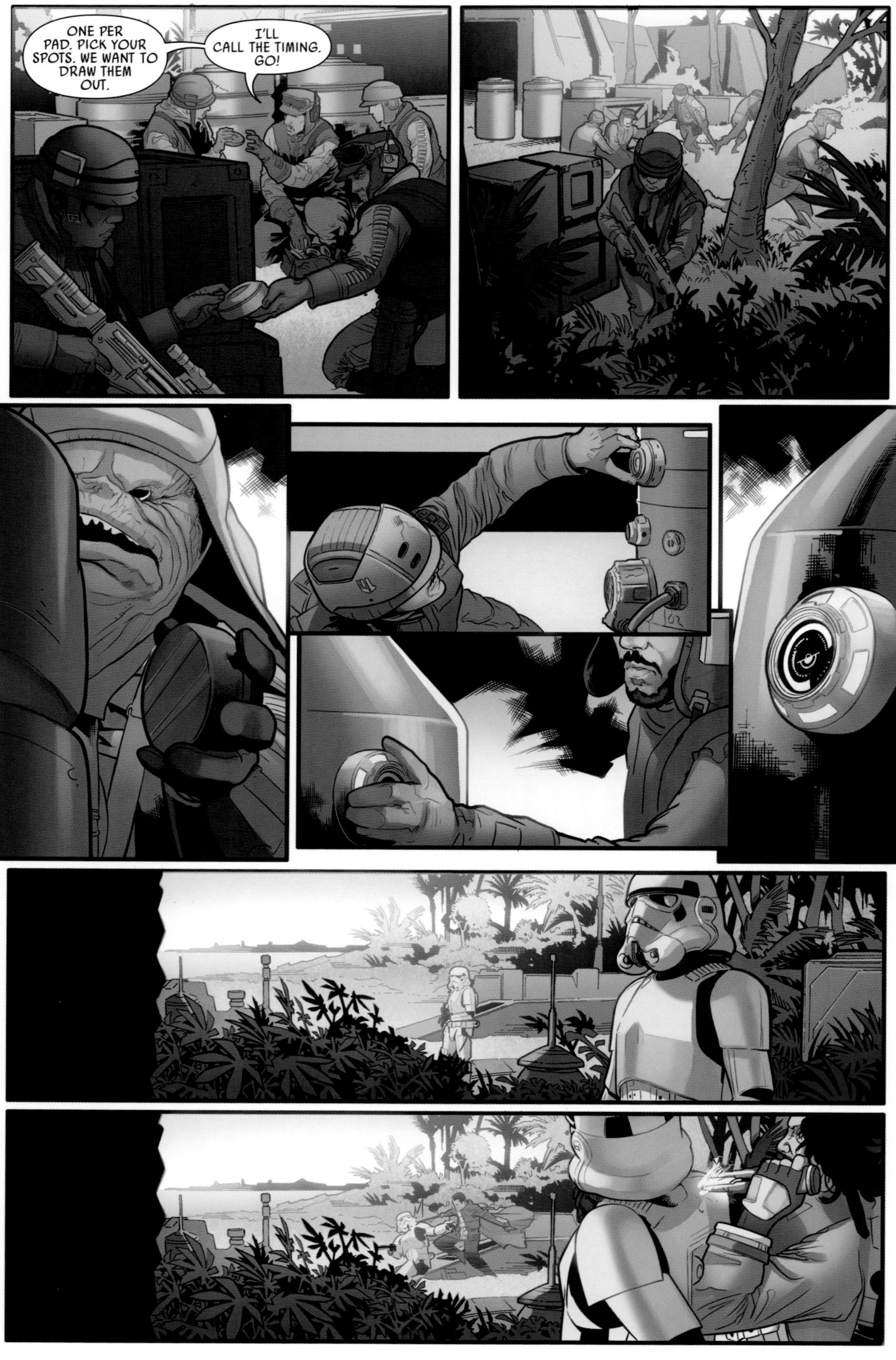
ONE PER PAD. PICK YOUR SPOTS. WE WANT TO DRAW THEM OUT.
I'LL CALL THE TIMING. GO!

EXCUSE ME. MAY I REQUEST YOUR ASSISTANCE?

WITH WHAT?

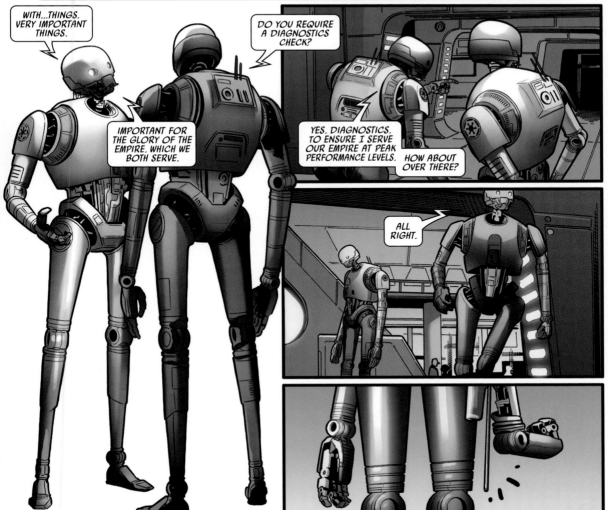

WITH...THINGS. VERY IMPORTANT THINGS.

IMPORTANT FOR THE GLORY OF THE EMPIRE, WHICH WE BOTH SERVE.

DO YOU REQUIRE A DIAGNOSTICS CHECK?

YES. DIAGNOSTICS. TO ENSURE I SERVE OUR EMPIRE AT PEAK PERFORMANCE LEVELS. HOW ABOUT OVER THERE?

ALL RIGHT.

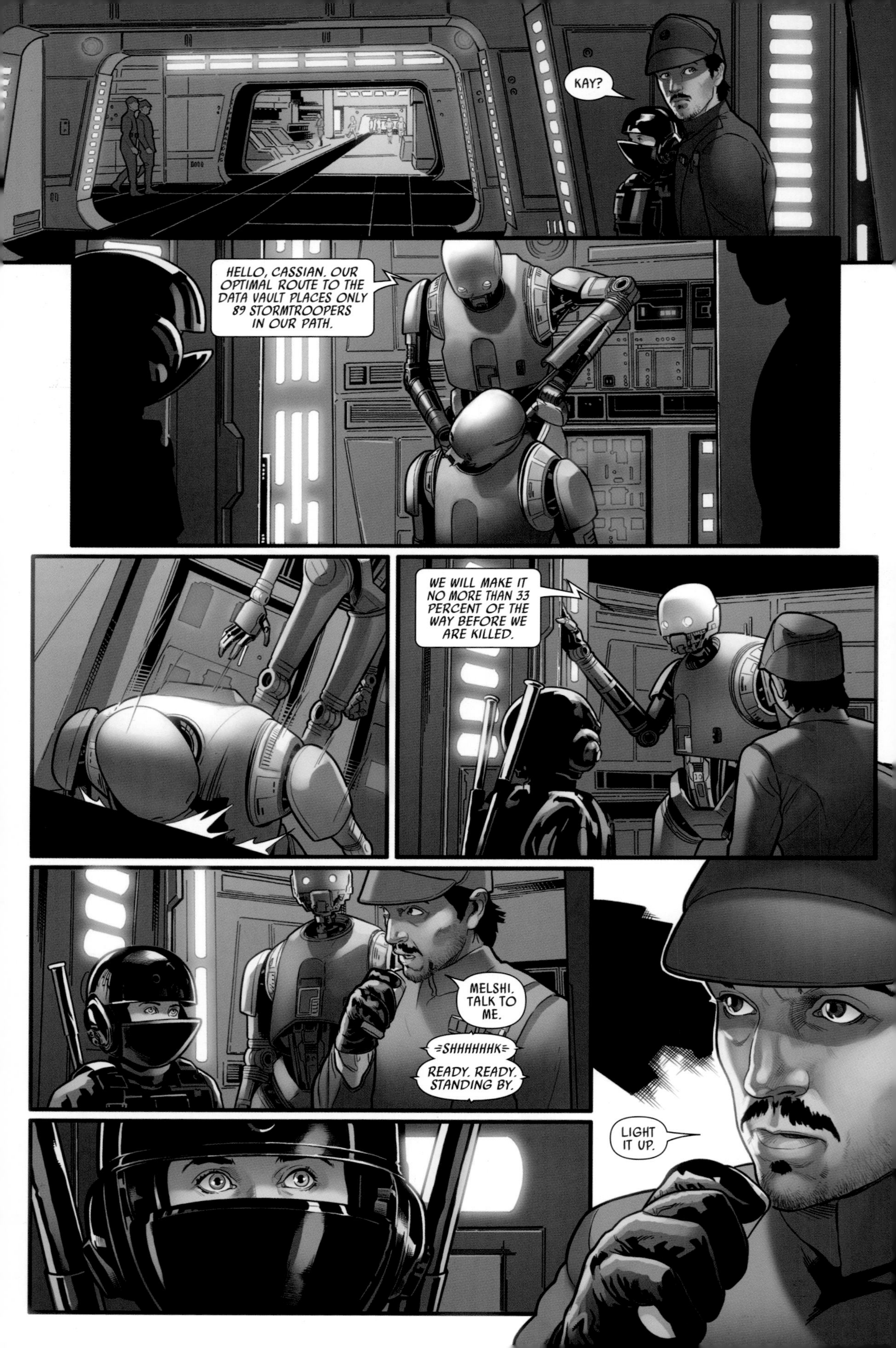
KAY?
HELLO, CASSIAN. OUR OPTIMAL ROUTE TO THE DATA VAULT PLACES ONLY 89 STORMTROOPERS IN OUR PATH.
WE WILL MAKE IT NO MORE THAN 33 PERCENT OF THE WAY BEFORE WE ARE KILLED.
MELSHI. TALK TO ME.
SHHHHHHK
READY. READY. STANDING BY.
LIGHT IT UP.

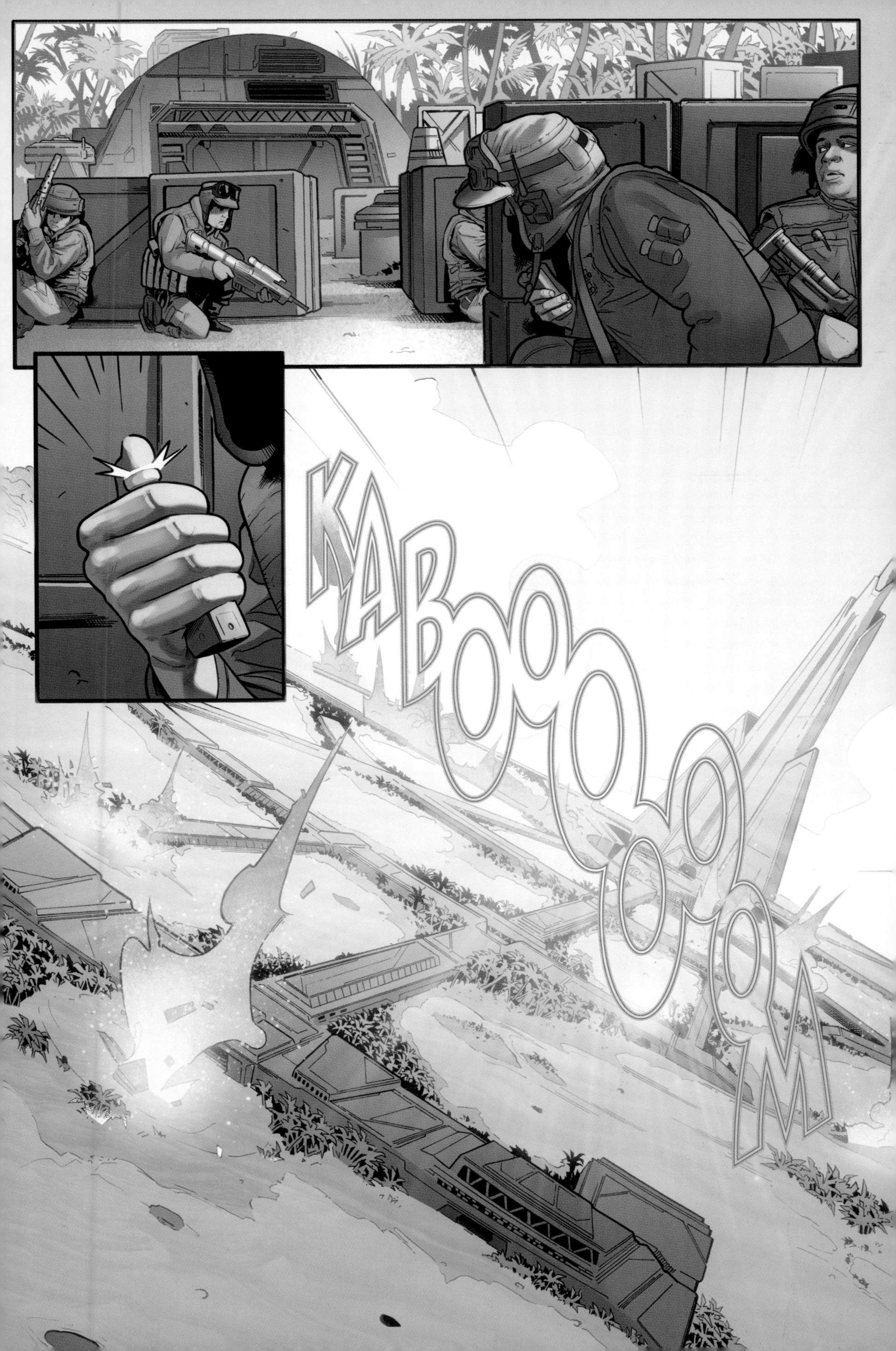
KABOOOOOOOOM

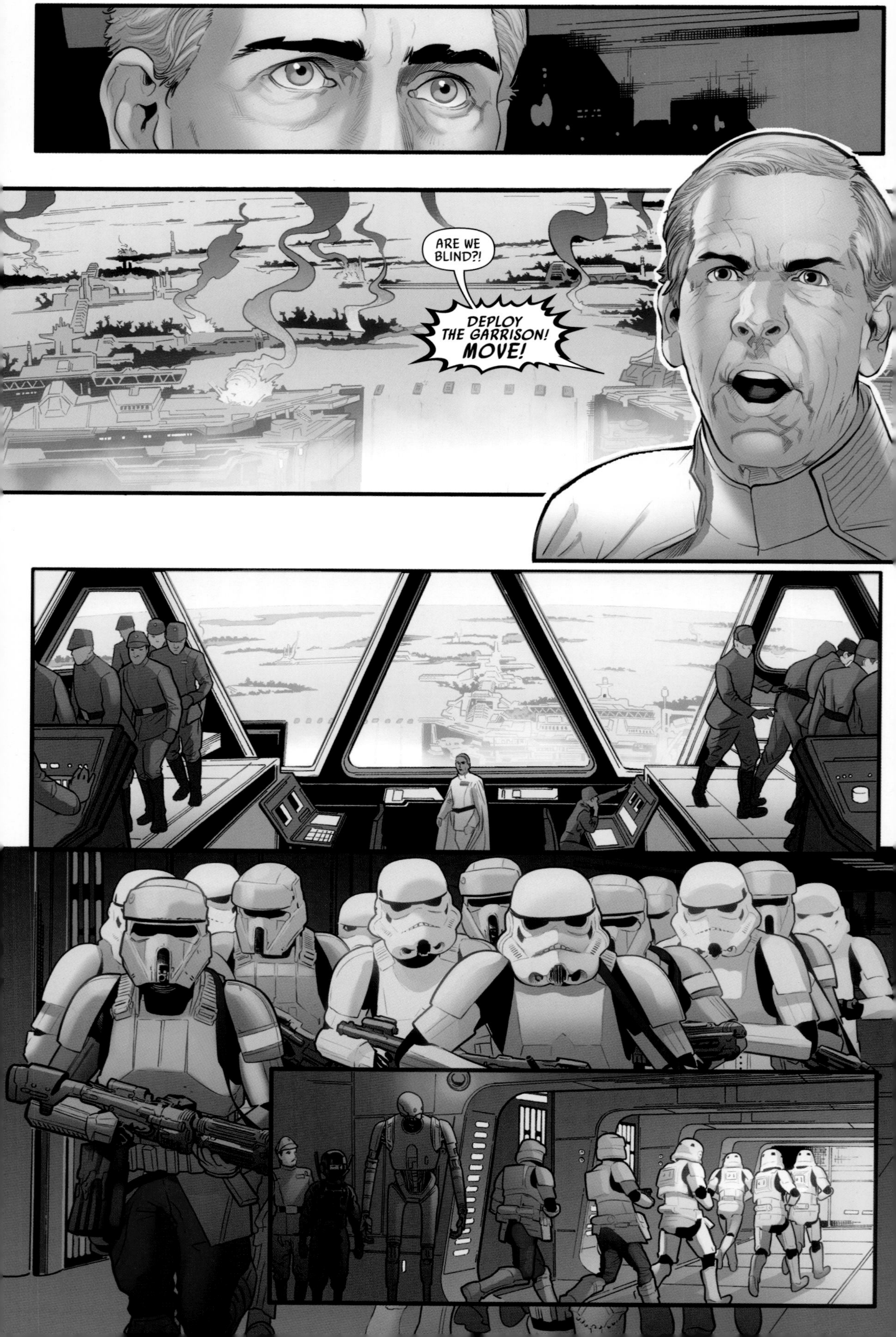
ARE WE BLIND?!
DEPLOY THE GARRISON! MOVE!

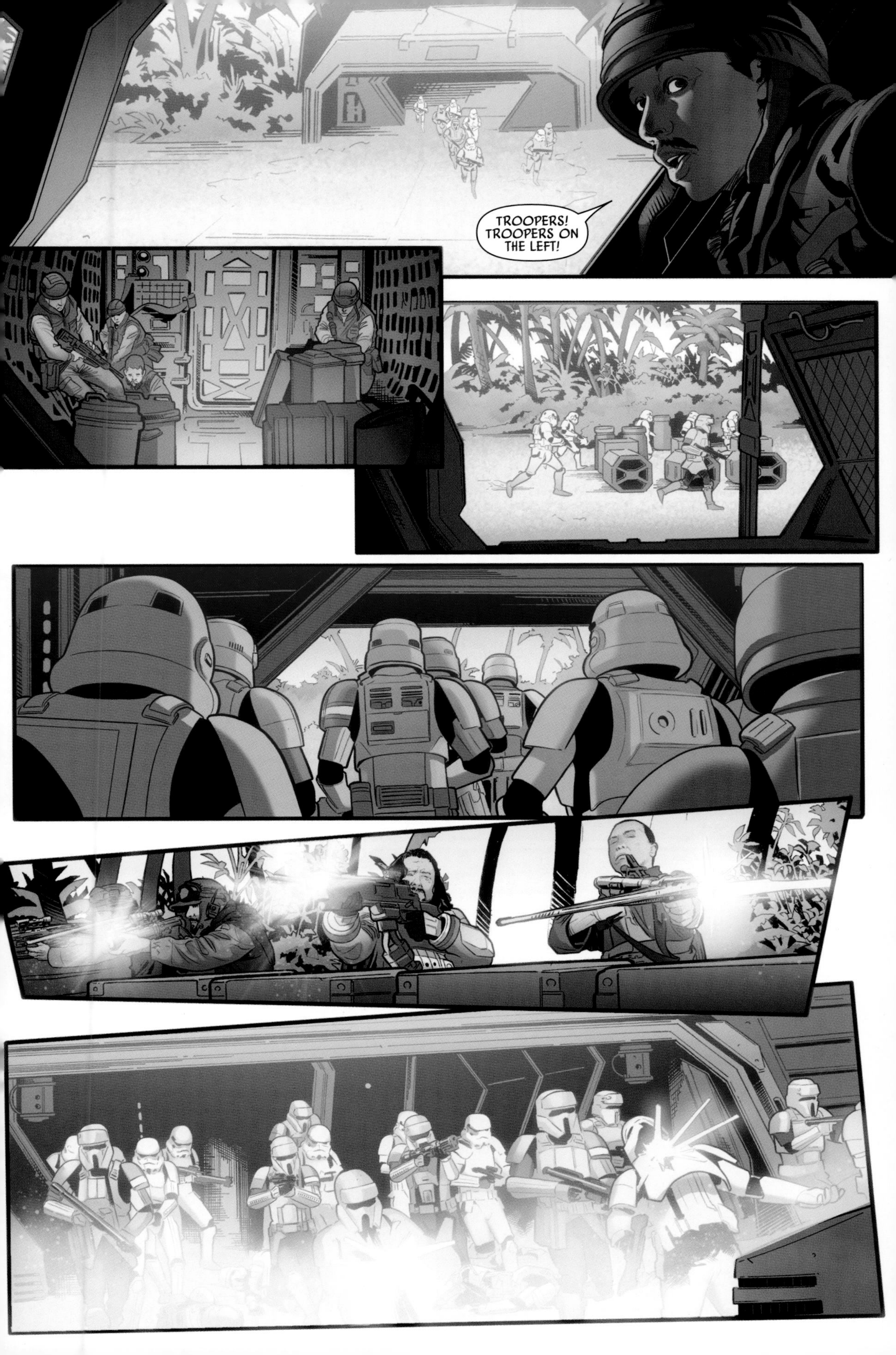
TROOPERS! TROOPERS ON THE LEFT!

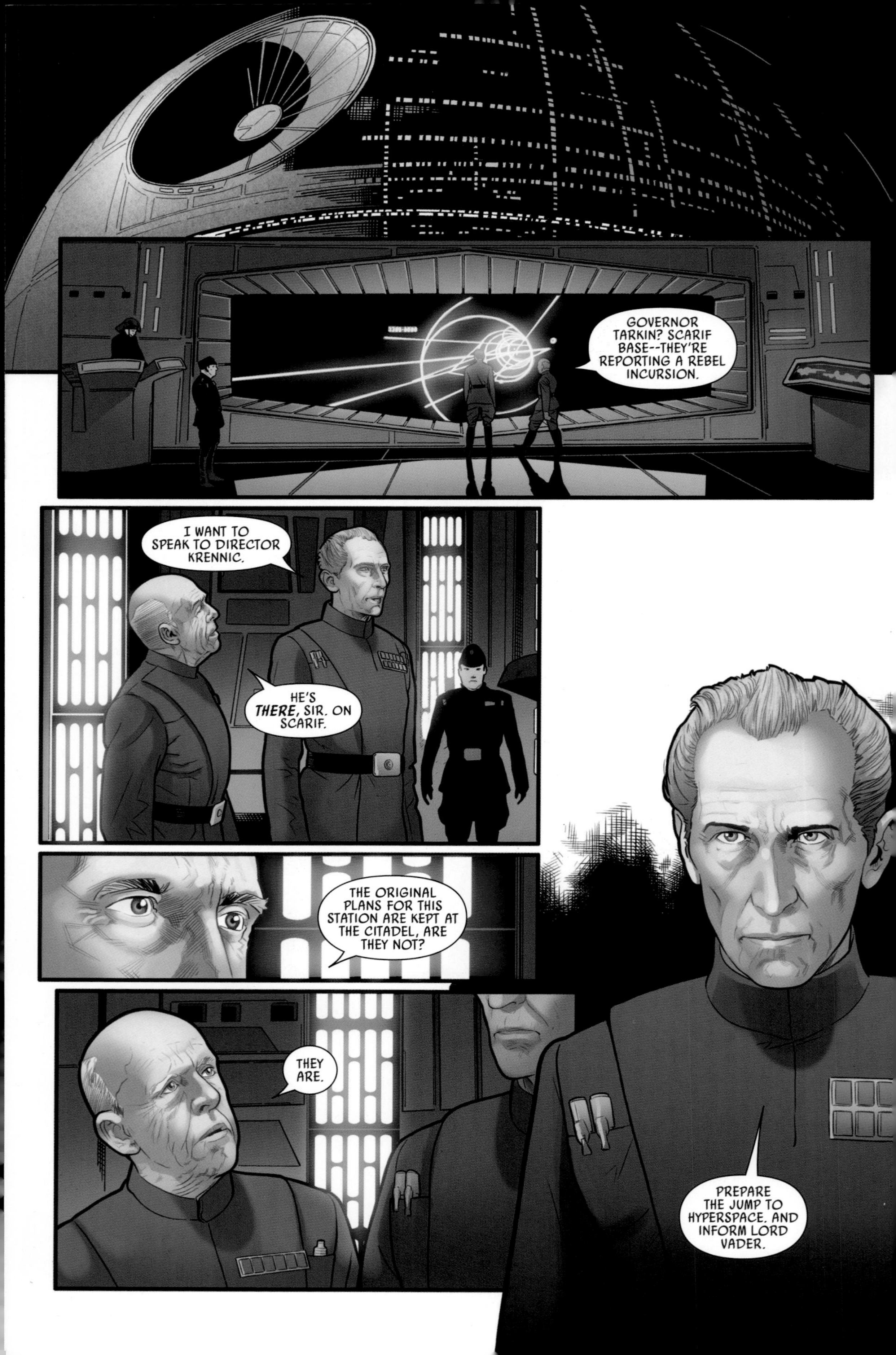
GOVERNOR TARKIN? SCARIF BASE--THEY'RE REPORTING A REBEL INCURSION.
I WANT TO SPEAK TO DIRECTOR KRENNIC.
HE'S *THERE*, SIR. ON SCARIF.
THE ORIGINAL PLANS FOR THIS STATION ARE KEPT AT THE CITADEL, ARE THEY NOT?
THEY ARE.
PREPARE THE JUMP TO HYPERSPACE. AND INFORM LORD VADER.

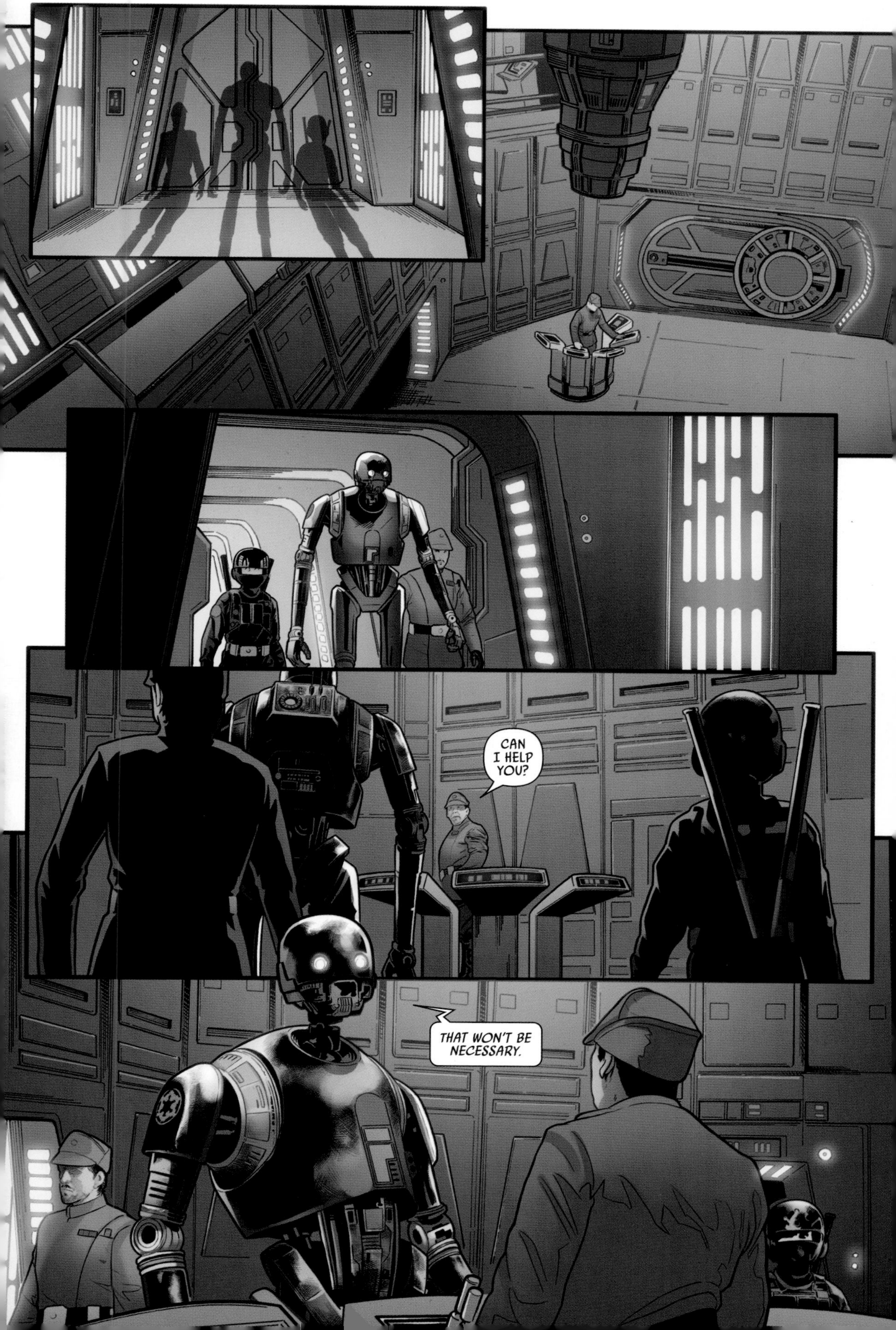
CAN I HELP YOU?
THAT WON'T BE NECESSARY.

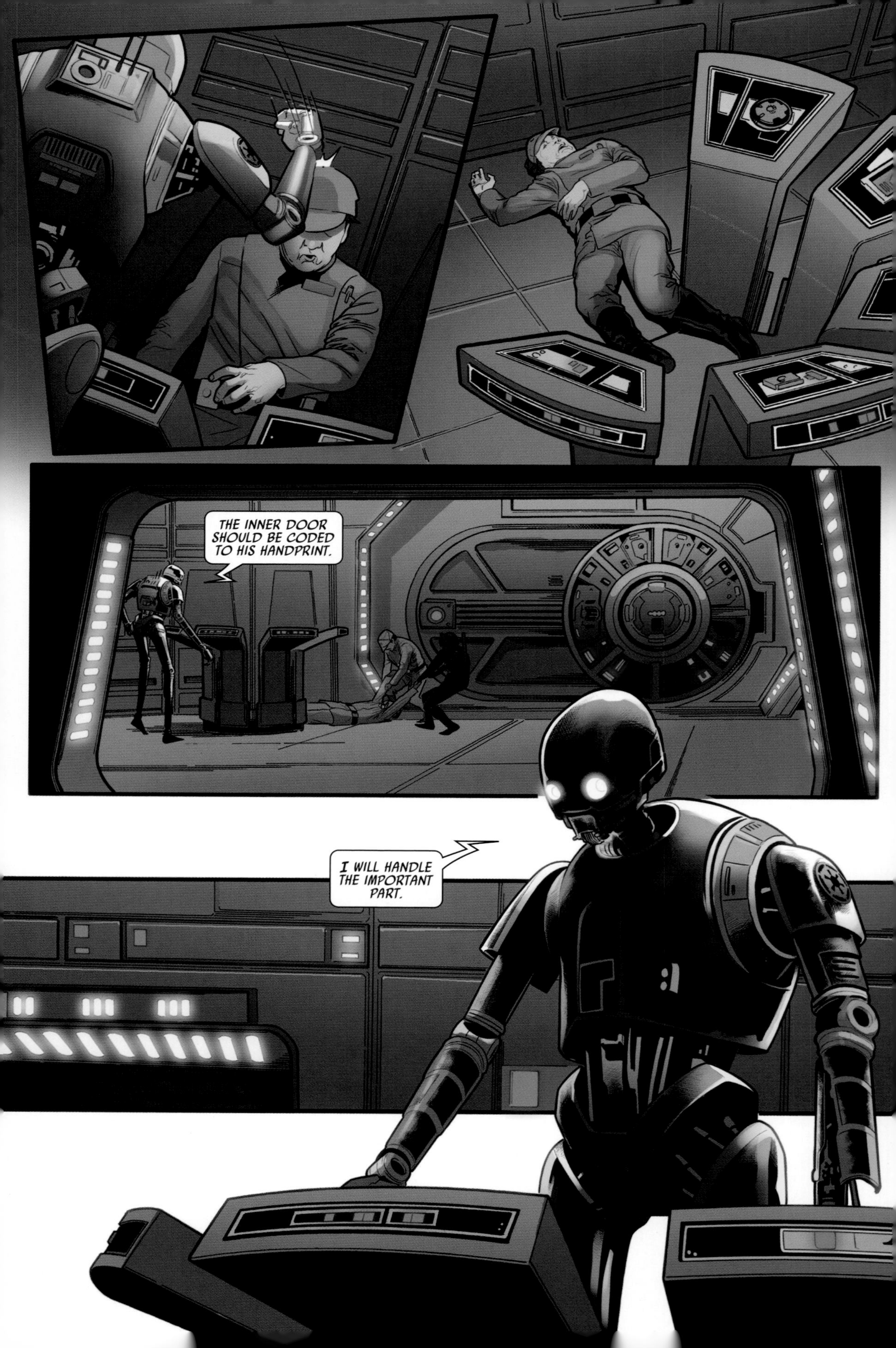
THE INNER DOOR SHOULD BE CODED TO HIS HANDPRINT.
I WILL HANDLE THE IMPORTANT PART.

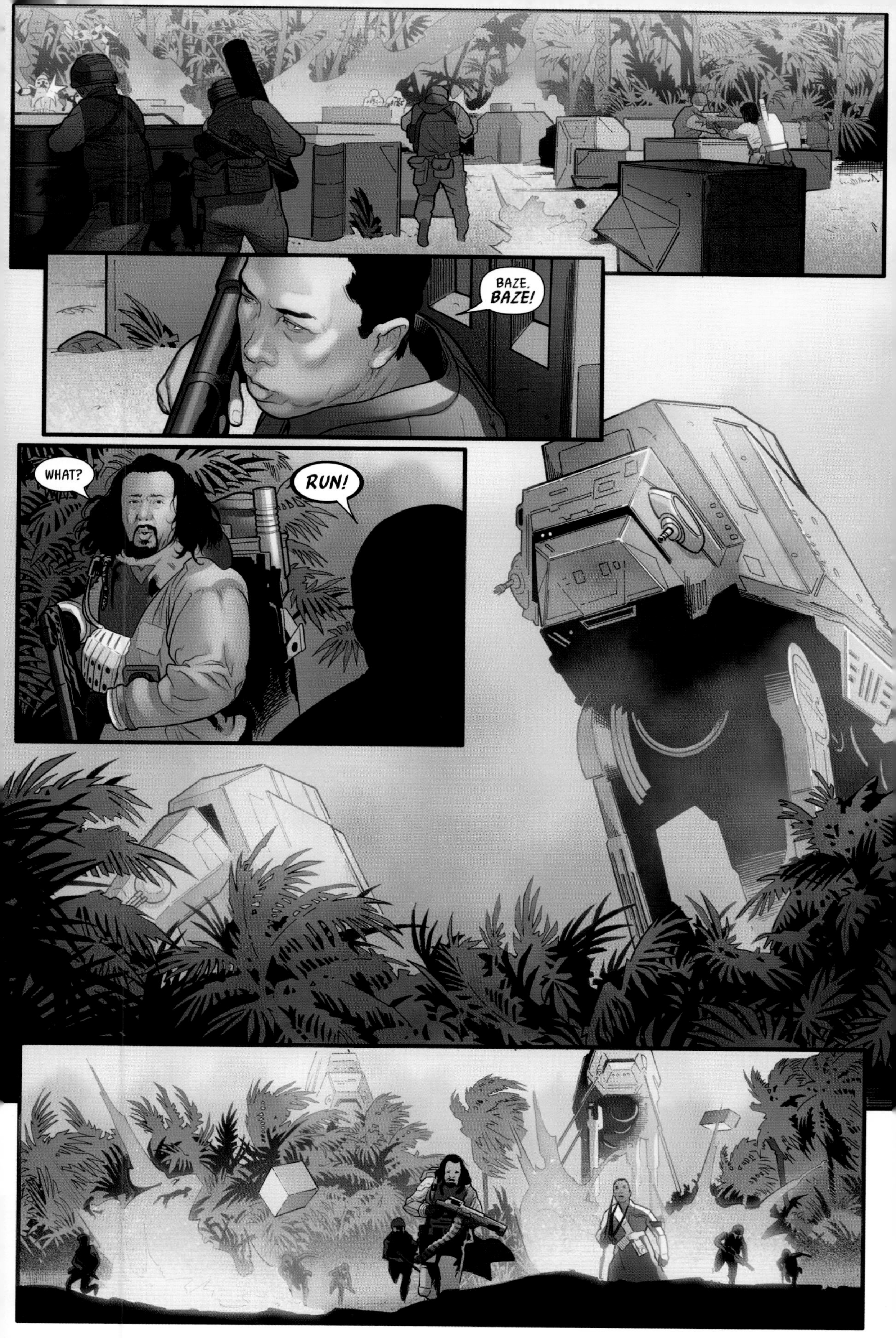
BAZE.
BAZE!
WHAT?
RUN!

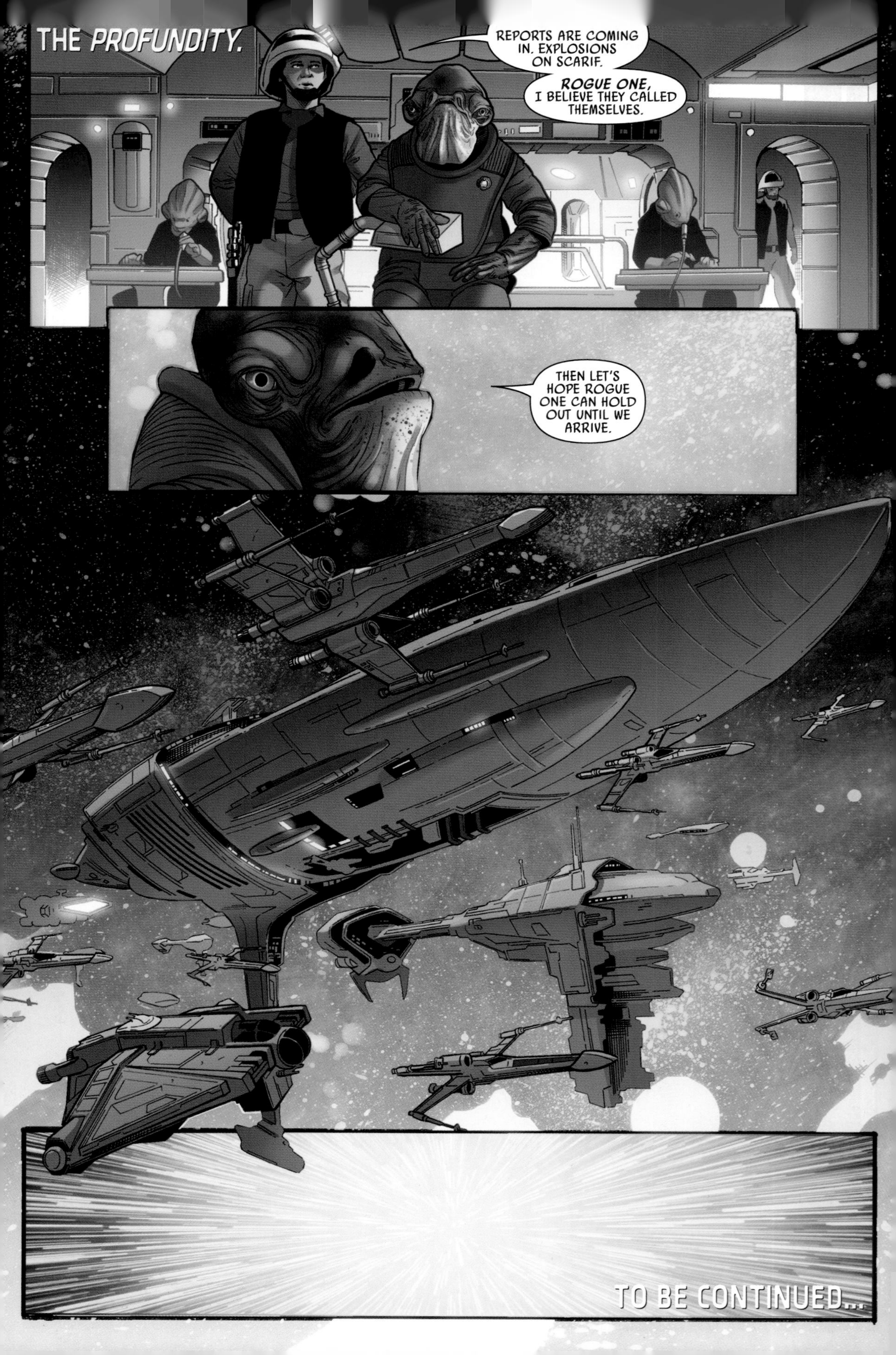
THE *PROFUNDITY.*
REPORTS ARE COMING IN. EXPLOSIONS ON SCARIF.
ROGUE ONE, I BELIEVE THEY CALLED THEMSELVES.
THEN LET'S HOPE ROGUE ONE CAN HOLD OUT UNTIL WE ARRIVE.
TO BE CONTINUED...

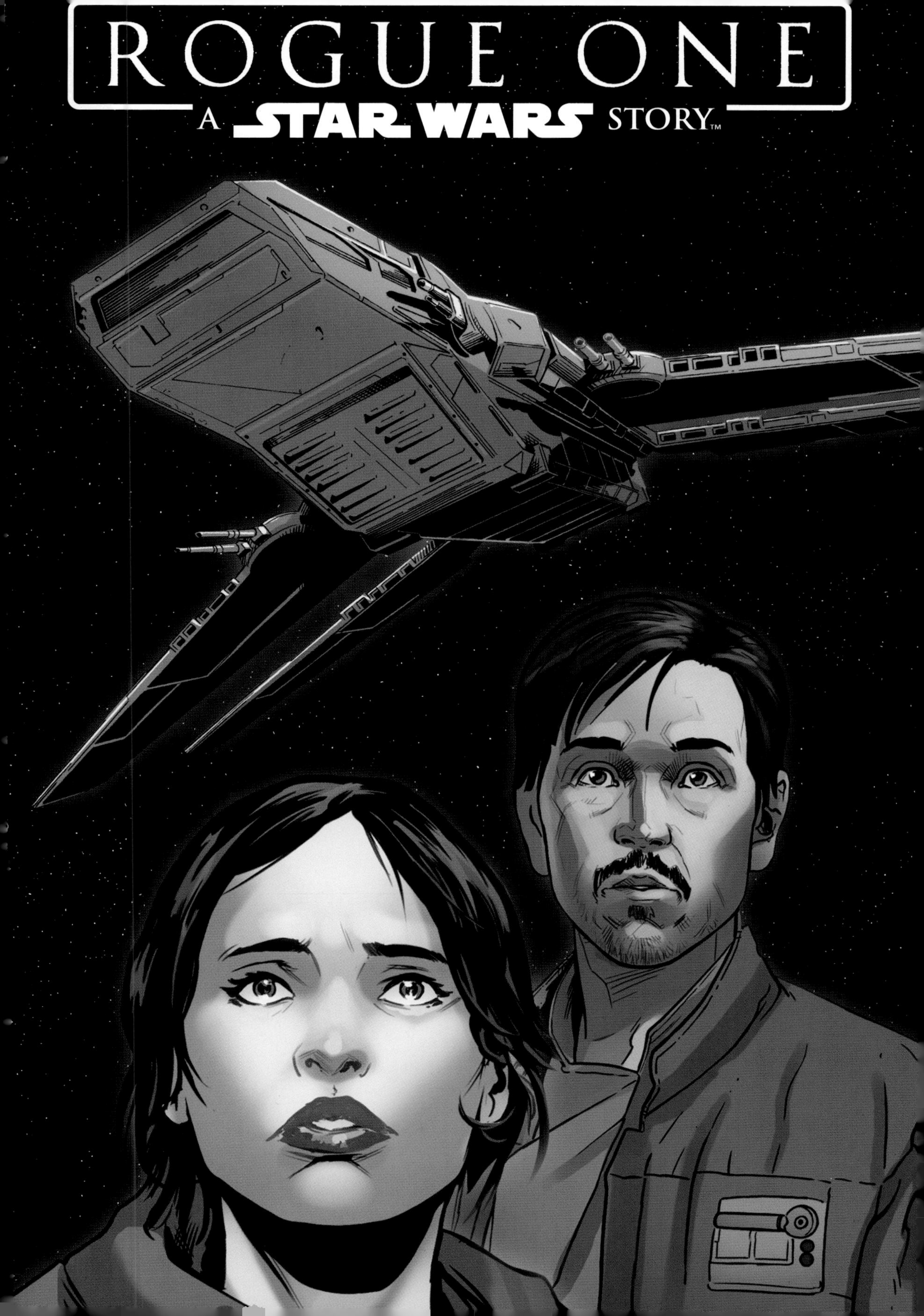
ROGUE ONE
A STAR WARS STORY™

ROGUE ONE
A STAR WARS STORY™

COLLECT THEM ALL!
Set of 6 Hardcover Books ISBN: 978-1-5321-4167-6

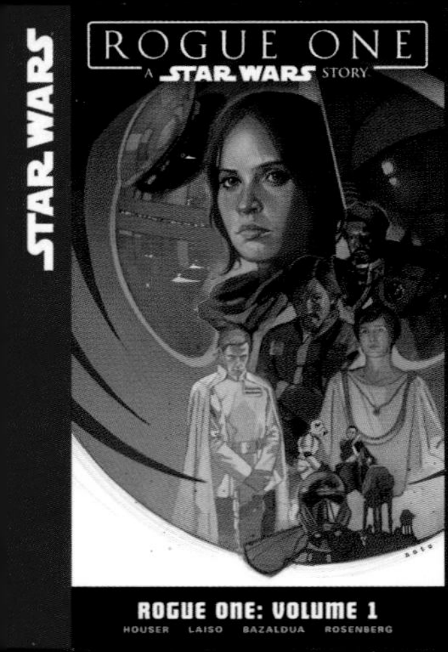
STAR WARS
ROGUE ONE
A STAR WARS STORY
ROGUE ONE: VOLUME 1
HOUSER LAISO BAZALDUA ROSENBERG

Hardcover Book ISBN
978-1-5321-4168-3

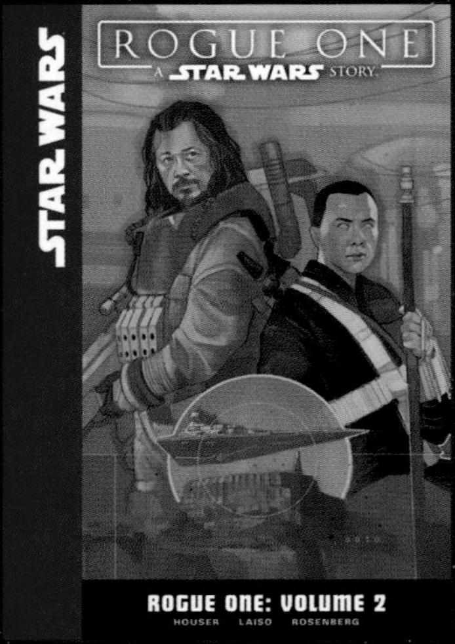
STAR WARS
ROGUE ONE
A STAR WARS STORY
ROGUE ONE: VOLUME 2
HOUSER LAISO ROSENBERG

Hardcover Book ISBN
978-1-5321-4169-0

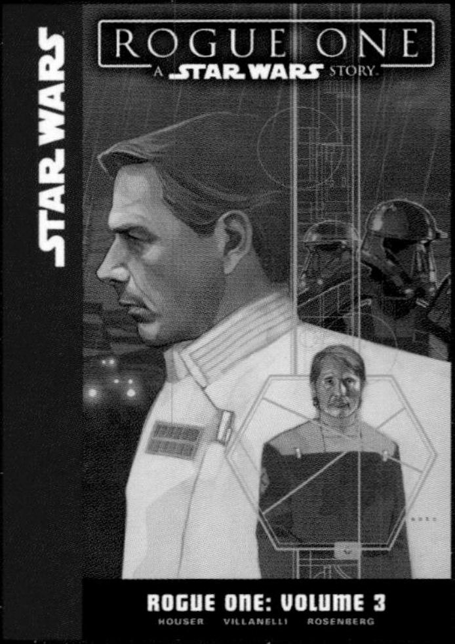
STAR WARS
ROGUE ONE
A STAR WARS STORY
ROGUE ONE: VOLUME 3
HOUSER VILLANELLI ROSENBERG

Hardcover Book ISBN
978-1-5321-4170-6

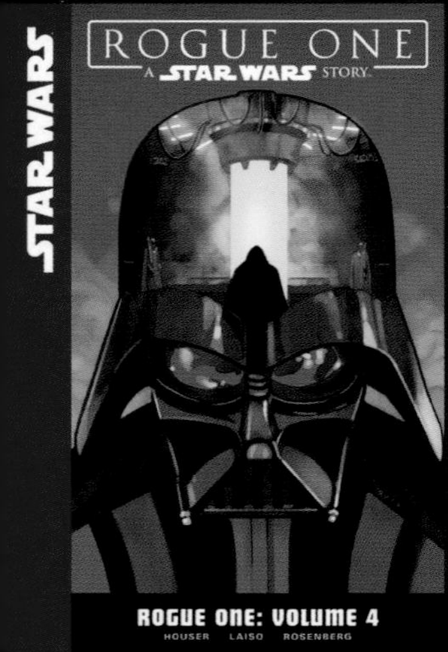
STAR WARS
ROGUE ONE
A STAR WARS STORY
ROGUE ONE: VOLUME 4
HOUSER LAISO ROSENBERG

Hardcover Book ISBN
978-1-5321-4171-3

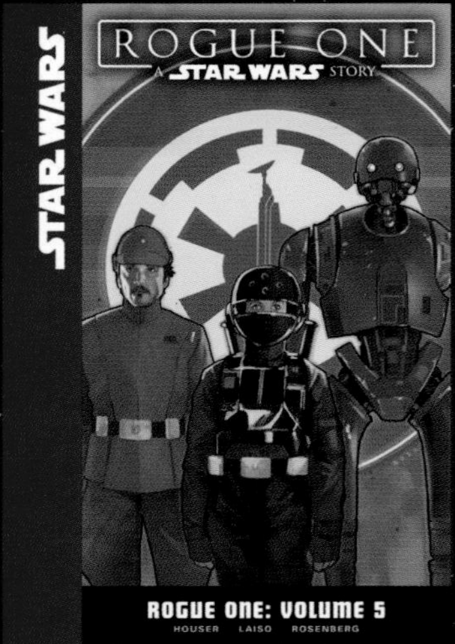
STAR WARS
ROGUE ONE
A STAR WARS STORY
ROGUE ONE: VOLUME 5
HOUSER LAISO ROSENBERG

Hardcover Book ISBN
978-1-5321-4172-0

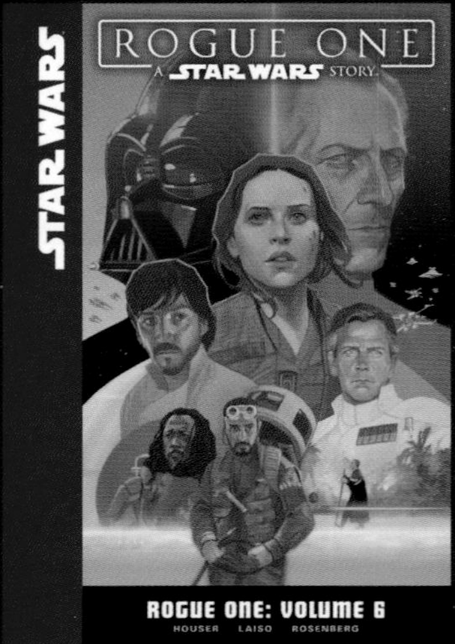
STAR WARS
ROGUE ONE
A STAR WARS STORY
ROGUE ONE: VOLUME 6
HOUSER LAISO ROSENBERG

Hardcover Book ISBN
978-1-5321-4173-7